from ancient India

ONCE
A MOUSE ...

a fable cut in wood

by MARCIA BROWN

ATHENEUM BOOKS FOR
YOUNG READERS

TO HILDA

Atheneum Books for Young Readers
An imprint of Simon & Schuster Children's Publishing Division
1230 Avenue of the Americas
New York, New York 10020
Copyright © 1961 by Marcia Brown

Printed in Hong Kong

33   35——34   32

Library of Congress Catalog Card Number 61-14769
ISBN 0-684-12662-1

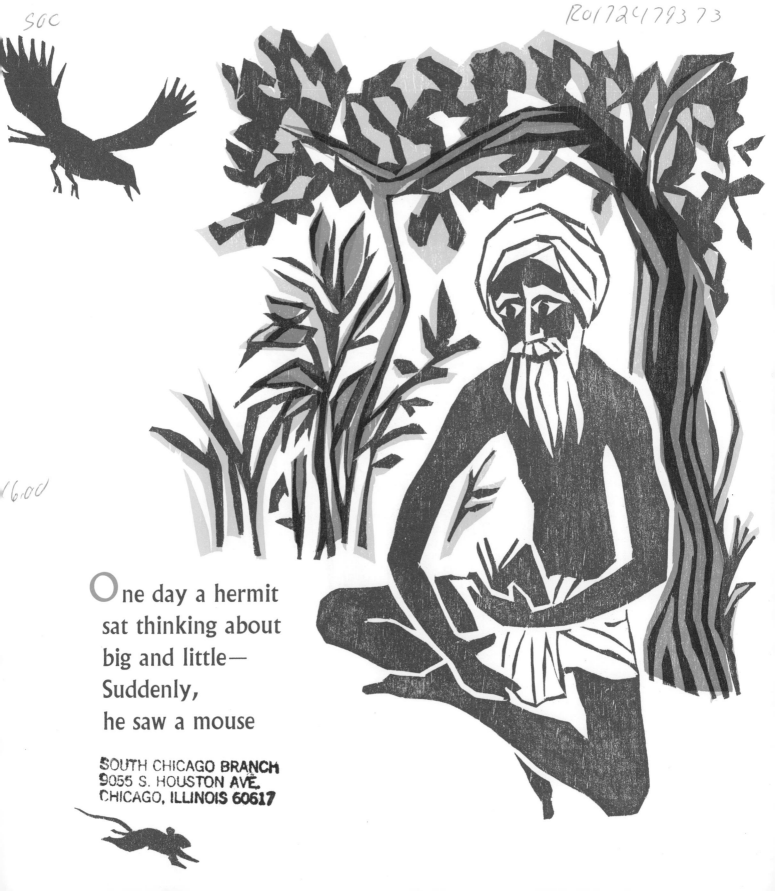

One day a hermit
sat thinking about
big and little—
Suddenly,
he saw a mouse

about to be snatched up by a crow.

He hurried

to help the poor little animal, and tearing him from the crow's greedy beak, he carried him off to

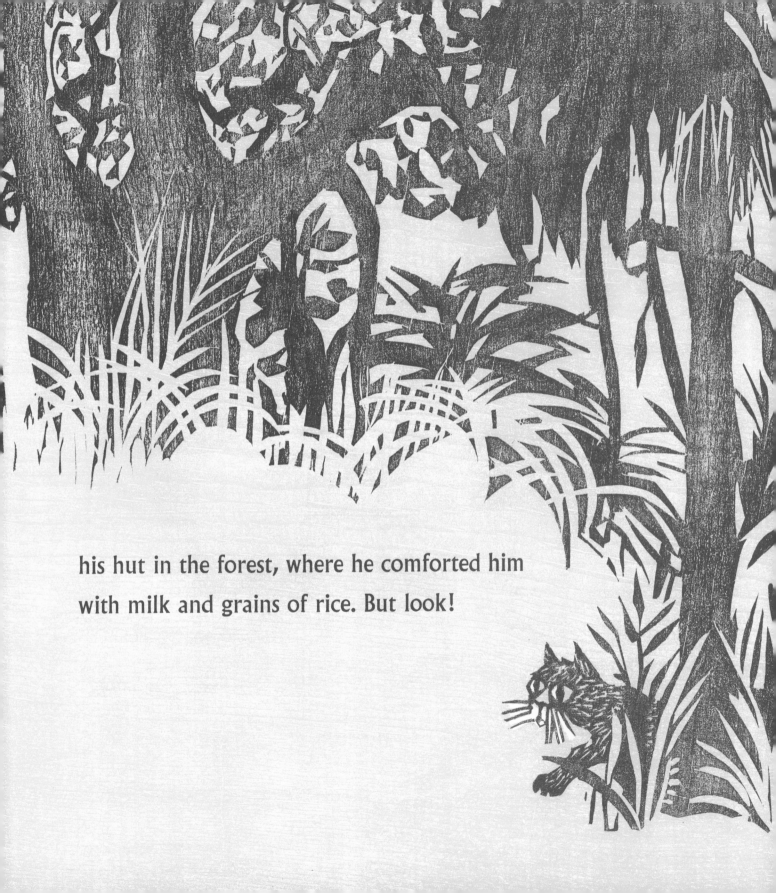

his hut in the forest, where he comforted him
with milk and grains of rice. But look!

A cat came to the hut with whiskers

straight and tail held high.

But the hermit was mighty at magic as well as at prayer.
When he saw the danger threatening his little pet, he
quickly changed him into a stout cat. But . . .

that night a dog barked in the forest.
Poor puss ran to hide under the bed. The
hermit wasted no time in thinking about
how big or so big, and

changed the cat into a big dog. Not long after that,
a hungry tiger

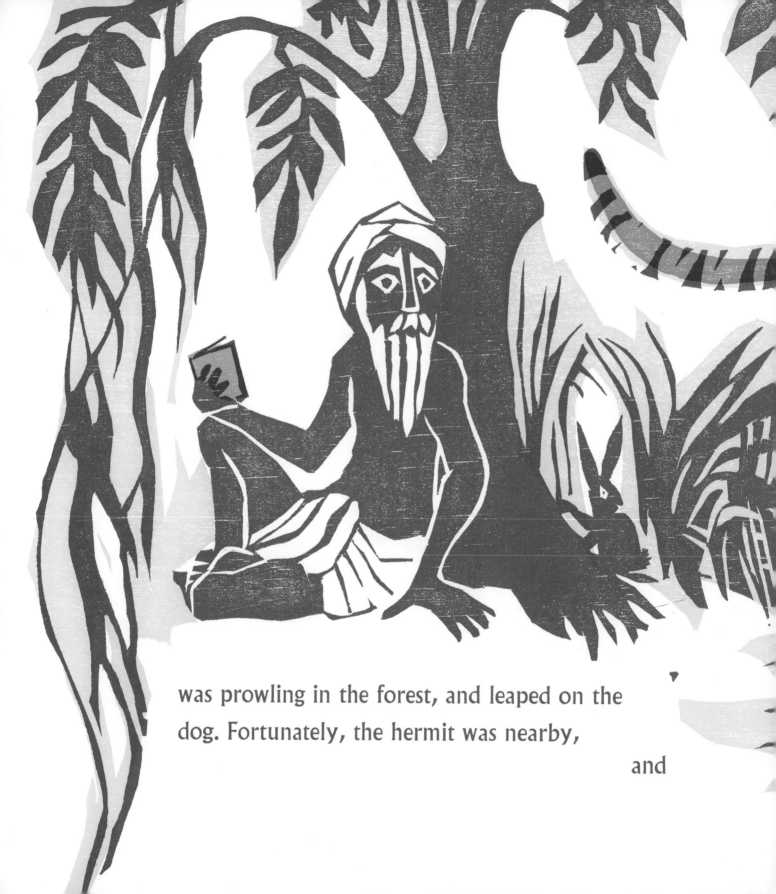

was prowling in the forest, and leaped on the
dog. Fortunately, the hermit was nearby,

and

with a gesture, he changed the dog

into a handsome, royal tiger. Now,

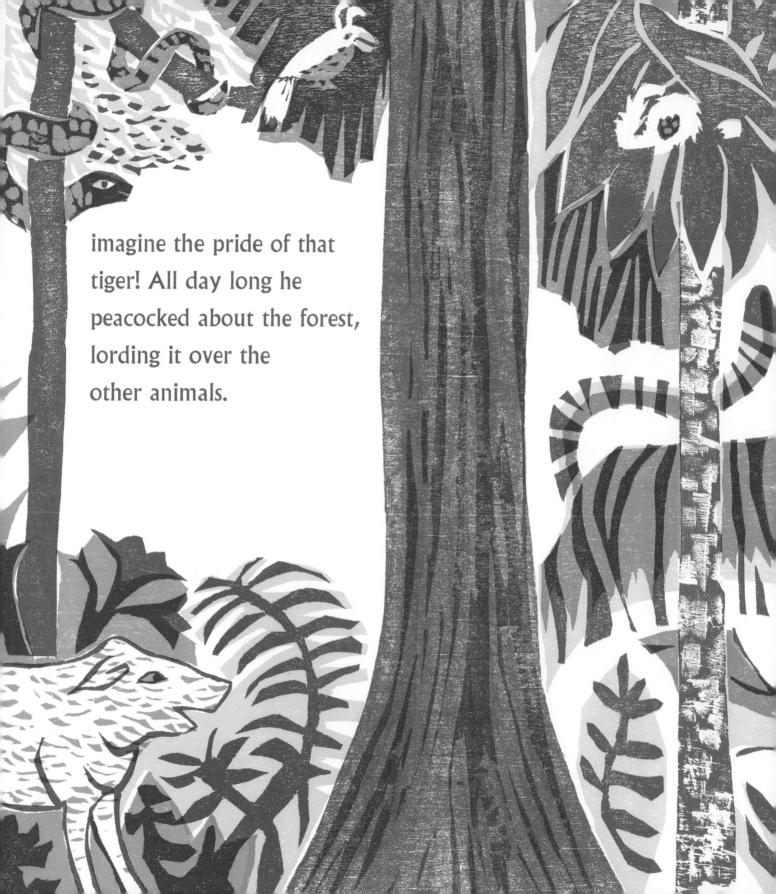

imagine the pride of that tiger! All day long he peacocked about the forest, lording it over the other animals.

The hermit missed nothing of all this, and chided the beast. "Without me," he would say to him, "you would be a wretched little mouse, that is, if you were still alive. There is no need to give yourself such airs."

The tiger felt offended and humiliated. He forgot
all the good he had received from the old man.

"No one shall tell me that I was once a mouse.
I will kill him!"

But the hermit read the tiger's mind.
"You are ungrateful! Go back to the forest and
be a mouse again!"
So the proud and handsome tiger turned back
into a frightened, humble, little mouse,

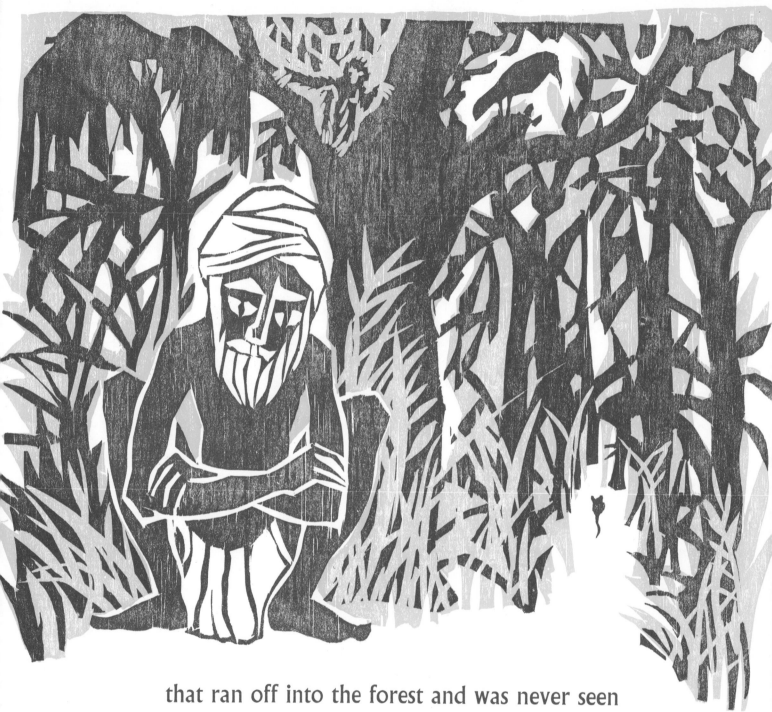

that ran off into the forest and was never seen
again. And the hermit sat thinking about big—
and little . . .